For my mom and dad —M.T.

For my Appa, who allowed me to dream —S.K.

Author's Note

A migrant worker is someone who moves from one part of the country to another—or between countries—to find work. They leave their hometowns and settle in and around cities to find jobs that pay more than what they would earn in rural towns. In China, nearly 300 million people (almost the entire population of the United States of America) are considered migrant workers.

Life for migrant workers is often difficult. They typically work long hours doing manual labor. You might see migrant workers (sometimes referred to as "day laborers") on construction and demolition sites, or working on farms and in gardens.

Migrant workers often save money to care for their elders and extended family members. For some, the money allows them to retire to their lǎo jiā 老家 ("old home"). For many migrant workers, the goal is to create a better life for their children.

"Iron rice bowl" is a Chinese term for a secure job with a steady income.

Peaches in Chinese culture symbolize a long and healthy life.

Text copyright © 2024 by Marie Tang
Jacket art and interior illustrations copyright © 2024 by Seo Kim

Visit us on the Web! rhcbooks.com

Educators and librarians, for a variety of teaching tools, visit us at RHTeachersLibrarians.com

Library of Congress Cataloging-in-Publication Data is available upon request.
ISBN 978-0-593-56507-0 (trade) — ISBN 978-0-593-56508-7 (lib. bdg.) — ISBN 978-0-593-56509-4 (ebook)

The illustrations in this book were created digitally.
The text of this book is set in 17-point Calluna Regular.
Interior design by Rachael Cole

MANUFACTURED IN CHINA
10 9 8 7 6 5 4 3 2 1
First Edition

Baba's Peach Tree

written by Marie Tang ✳ illustrated by Seo Kim

RANDOM HOUSE STUDIO 🏠 NEW YORK

In the deep green meadow behind our
old stone house stood a peach tree.

Every morning, Baba would wake
before the sun and water the tree.

"You see, Tao Hua, the things we
nourish always flourish," he would say.

Then across the fields and over the hills we went.
Baba would head to town, and I would continue
walking, counting the crop rows that led to my school.

On my way home, I scowled at the
books that weighed me down.
With cold hands and numbers on
my mind, all I wanted was to rest.

But Baba never said a word about how tired he was.

Baba pruned and tended to the tree when all I wanted was to chase the rooster and dip my feet in the stream.

He called the tree a blessing like
good shoes, hot rice, and books.

Day after day, we watched its branches reach to the heavens as its roots grew deep into the ground.

When the cold finally left, spring showers left a dewy sheen on our meadow.

Our tree's cloud of flowers turned magenta like the sky at dinnertime.

Nestled inside the petals of each flower was a tiny green bulb, shiny like a gem.

Summer came, and those jade-colored
pearls blossomed into peaches.
Big, fuzzy orange-pink globes, each
one kissed by the sun.

Long days were filled with games and
dancing around the tree's narrow trunk.
I sank my teeth into the juicy peaches
while honeybees chased me around the field.
Those were the best days.

But Baba would say, "There is work to do."

There was always work to do.

All summer long, Baba sold our peaches.

"Lai le, lai le! Come, come! Buy one, taste the sun,"
Baba shouted.

Every night, Baba handed me a peach as big as his
hand. He always saved the best one for me.

After I finished my peach, I would go out
to the field behind the stone house, press its
wrinkly pit into the soil, and make a wish.

Some days, I wished for rain.

Some days, I wished for an extra bowl of rice.

But mostly, I wished to see Baba smile.

Time passed, and the seasons brought change of all kinds.
Sometimes our peach tree grew tall and proud.
And sometimes it sagged and swayed with the wind.
Hot days that turned into cold nights made me shiver too.

Then one year, our peach tree did not blossom at all.
The green leaves that once cradled the jade nuggets turned
yellow and kowtowed to the ground.

"What happened, Baba?"

"Everything has its time, Tao Hua. The peach tree has
no more fruit to give."

That summer, we said goodbye to our peach fortune.

Winter came, and Baba worked extra hard.

I watched Baba's odd jobs turn into night jobs. Some even turned into overnight jobs.

Those were the loneliest days.

One day, Baba came home and shouted,
"Our iron rice bowl has finally come!"
Baba got a job in the Big City.
I didn't want to leave the old stone house,
but he said there were good schools in the city.

For many moons, we lived in a concrete building, and
Baba worked in a dusty place that didn't have peach sun.

Then, like our old tree, I blossomed too.

The years passed.
Baba grew old and frail.

I took Baba back to the place
where our peach tree once grew.

In the deep green meadow behind the
old stone house, a rainbow of pink and red
reached high into the sky.